MOVING!

"Moving?" Molly gasped. She didn't even like saying that word out loud. "I don't want to move. Why can't I stay here with all my friends?"

Molly's parents didn't even try to answer that question.

"Why does Grandpa have to be sick anyway?" Molly blurted out. "It's all his fault!"

Now she was really going to get a talking-to, the one about disappointing her parents and just thinking about herself.

She knew what happened when people moved. People forgot all about you. Like her best friend in nursery school, Kristin, who moved away. Now she didn't even remember Kristin's last name.

There had to be a way to get her parents to take back their words. There just had to be!

P.S. We'll Miss You
Yours 'Til the Meatball Bounces
2 Sweet 2 B 4-Gotten
Remember Me, When This You See

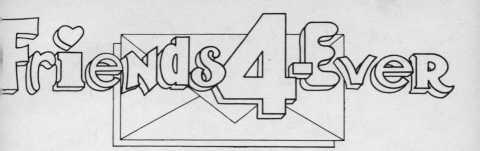

P.S. WE'LL MISS YOU

Deirdre Corey

AN
APPLE
PAPERBACK

SCHOLASTIC INC.
New York Toronto London Auckland Sydney

To Molly O'Gorman —
we miss you

MOLLY'S BAD NEWS

Molly Quindlen was sitting up in bed. Balanced against her knees was a clipboard holding long strands of colored string. Black. Turquoise. White. Yellow. Molly knew exactly which strings went over and which went under. Her dad always said she had sharp eyes. Good thing, since she was weaving the ankle bracelet in a dim triangle of light coming from the hallway.

She was supposed to be asleep.

Molly and her friends were all learning how to make braided wrist and ankle bracelets, just like the ones all the middle-school girls wore.

"We'll never take them off, not even when we're twenty," Laura announced just that morning in the car pool on the way to day camp.

The four girls — Laura, Meg, Stevie, and Molly, of course — brought their clipboards and bags of colored string everywhere, including to bed. All the mothers said they were going to ruin their eyesight, but the girls didn't care.

"So what? We'll all get glasses together. Cool ones," they cried whenever they heard this.

Now Molly wanted to finish one last inch of the V-stitch pattern Meg said was too hard. Well, just because Meg Milano was seven months older than the other three girls didn't make her the world expert on the V-stitch. In fact, Meg's comments just made Molly more determined to have that bracelet around her ankle by the next morning at the latest. She could just picture herself stretching her right leg across the backseat for the whole car pool to see.

Suddenly, a shadow cut off the light Molly needed to finish the job.

"Molly! I thought you were asleep," her mother interrupted. "You know how hard it is for you to get up in the morning."

Molly shoved her clipboard of strings under

2

the covers and tried to make her big brown eyes look sleepy. It was no use.

"I'm not tired! Besides, you promised you would help me finish the comb case so I can give it to Daddy for his birthday." There. Now they could talk about that instead of bedtime.

The more Molly thought about it, the madder she got. Lately her mother was *always* forgetting her promises. Her parents seemed to be talking and whispering all the time when they were supposed to be taking Molly and Scotty out for ice cream, or punching holes in mayonnaise jars for fireflies, or helping make birthday presents, for example.

Molly got herself all fired up for another going-to-bed fight.

"Well, as long as you're up, I'll go get Daddy. I asked him to come up with me if you were still awake."

Molly forgot all about her string and about being mad. The only time her parents came into her room together at night was when she was sick or to give her a talking-to.

What was it this time? She sure hoped it wasn't another baby. She already had a little brother and definitely didn't need another one.

And she'd gone for two whole days without calling Scotty Snake Brain or Scaredy Pants. So it couldn't be that. They weren't going to get rid of Riggs, were they? Molly remembered how they had both sat on the edge of her bed to tell her they had to give away their cat, Marmalade, just because of Scotty's allergies. Well it wasn't going to happen to her dog. She'd run away with Riggs first!

Molly pulled the sides of the pillow tight around her ears, flattening her straight brown hair against her head. She didn't let go, even when she saw her parents in the doorway. Whatever they had to tell her, she wasn't going to listen.

Her dad pulled her hands away from the pillow.

"Hey, Molly Melinda," he said quietly.

Mr. Quindlen looked at her for an awfully long time. Molly felt hot, and her ears were buzzing inside.

"Want to see my ankle bracelet, Daddy? Meg said the V-stitch was too hard but I'm almost finished and I'm going to wear it to camp tomorrow and I only have another inch to go."

Molly scrambled under the sheets to find the bracelet.

"Whoa, slow down, Molly. Why don't you show it to me in the morning?" Mr. Quindlen said when she came up for air. Molly fell back on her pile of pillows, three fat pillows to be exact, all plumped up in a certain way so she could fall asleep.

Mr. Quindlen pulled up the mound of covers, the blue ones with the white sheep that Molly also couldn't sleep without. He smoothed the sheets around her, nice and straight. Reaching over a pile of books, a tissue box, and a plastic cup of water, Mr. Quindlen turned on the balloon lamp, and the room glowed in its soft light.

It must be Grandpa, thought Molly. That was it. He'd been sick. What if he died? Molly got that same feeling she used to get when Marmalade sat on her chest. But a very tiny part of her didn't feel that way. A little part of her was relieved that this probably wasn't about Riggs. Her parents would never get rid of the best part-Schnauzer in the world.

Something was definitely going on with Molly's parents. Otherwise, why was her mother putting Molly's old stuffed rabbit up on the shelf where it belonged instead of making Molly put it away?

Molly curled her toes the way she always did when she got nervous. She swallowed hard, and her ears popped.

"Did Grandpa die?"

Her parents looked at each other and smiled.

"No, Sweetpea, he didn't die. He's just sick, and he can't run the hardware store by himself anymore," her dad answered.

Since he didn't die, why were they all sitting in her room like that? Maybe her father was sad because there wasn't going to be a Quindlen's Hardware Store anymore. He was always telling Molly stories about when he was a little boy and had to weigh nails in a brown paper bag for the customers. Or the time he climbed on the rolling ladder and crashed into the mayor, who had come in for a plunger. Her dad's stories usually had some kind of lesson in them, like doing a good job or being responsible, but Molly liked hearing them anyway.

Molly looked at her dad's face. He didn't have that twinkle-in-his-eye look he usually got when he talked about growing up in Kansas. He looked kind of sad.

All of a sudden Molly felt sad, too. She thought about the hardware store, with all the shiny blank keys lined up in rows on a pegboard. And the cardboard boxes full of blue-green plastic gloves that Molly and Scotty liked to try on when they played Green Slime. There were boxes of orange soda-bottle stoppers, seven kinds of thermometers, cut-glass butter dishes, ceramic lazy Susans, and heavy wallpaper books Molly couldn't lift. Quindlen's Hardware had everything.

Molly stared at the wallpaper in her room. It had come from Quindlen's, and she had picked it out by herself. Creamy white paper with small pink houses on it. Molly turned away from her parents' serious faces and stared at the wall by her bed. She began tugging at a piece of wallpaper that began on a seam. This sometimes helped her get to sleep. But now she wasn't the least bit tired, just worried.

Her mother sat down on the corner of the bed and looked at Molly. "Honey, we have to go help Grandpa with the store."

"But what about Point o' Woods?" Molly asked in a much louder voice. The Quindlens usually went to the shore for the first two weeks of August, then to Kansas to visit Grandpa for another couple of weeks. But Kansas wasn't their real vacation. Vacation meant Point o' Woods and the beach. Molly had big plans this year. She was going to walk to the village by herself, and she was going to the high beach and swim in the surf, not at the baby bay beach anymore.

"Honey, we're all going to Grandpa's. Next month. To stay and help Grandpa," Mr. Quindlen said. He kept stroking the side of Molly's head, and her mother kept twisting the red sock Molly had forgotten, again, to put in the hamper.

"For a whole month? What about our real vacation?" Molly wailed, thinking about the list of things she had already written on her big calendar. The Point o' Woods Fair. Harbor Night. This year they were all going to go out on a whale-watching boat, too. She'd marked it all down, and now her parents were telling her there wasn't going to be any Point o' Woods.

Her parents kept looking around the room. Molly knew this talking-to wasn't over, if that's even what it was. She hadn't done anything bad, nothing she knew about anyway, but her parents were about to. She just had a feeling.

"We're moving to Kansas, Mol," her dad finally said. "For a year at least. Grandpa needs us to help out, to settle things at the store."

Molly kept staring at the wall. She pulled at the small piece of wallpaper again until she had torn off the roof of a pink house. Her pajamas felt all hot and twisted around her waist, and her brown bangs itched her forehead.

"Moving?" Molly gasped. She didn't even like saying that word out loud. "I don't want to move. Why can't I stay here with all my friends?"

Molly's parents didn't even try to answer that question.

"Why does Grandpa have to be sick anyway?" Molly blurted out. "It's all his fault!"

Now she was really going to get a talking-to, the one about disappointing her parents and just thinking about herself. Well, she didn't care. She just stuck her fingernail under the edge of another little pink house on the wall.

"Molly, turn over, hon," her father said, putting his hand on her shoulder. Molly made herself very skinny and very straight. A hot tear slid right down the sides of all three pillows.

Concentrating on the wall, Molly couldn't see her parents, but she could just picture them looking at each other the way they always did when something bad was already decided. Molly knew all the "Pleases" in the world wouldn't change their minds now. She pulled the covers over her shoulder even though she was roasting.

If only they hadn't said "moving." She knew what happened when people moved. People forgot all about you. Like her best friend in nursery school, Kristin, who moved away. Now she didn't even remember Kristin's last name.

"What about your job?" she asked her father between hiccups. Maybe her parents hadn't thought of that when they made all these plans about going to Kansas. Kansas! Molly knew exactly where it was on her beach ball globe. Kansas was at least six inches from the inky blob of Rhode Island, where she lived, and which didn't show up too well on the beach ball.

"The college said Daddy could take his year off now instead of next year. He can still work on his big paper out in Kansas," Mrs. Quindlen said softly.

Her mother's gentle voice. Her dad's gentle

face. None of it helped Molly right then. There had to be a way to get them to take back their words. There just had to be!

"What if they give his job to somebody else, and the students like that person better?" Molly asked, finally sitting up so her parents would really hear her. "Then he might not get his job back, and we won't have any mon —"

"Molly, we know how you feel, how hard it's going to be," her father said. "I wish we didn't have to do this. But it's only for a while."

"A year isn't a while!" Molly cried. "All my friends will forget about me. I'll be old when I get back. I won't get to be in the third-and-fourth-grade play or have extra recess."

"You won't be old when you get back, Mol," her dad said, trying to put his arms around her.

Molly pulled away. Her mind was spinning with so many panicked thoughts. She knew there were other good reasons why this moving-away plan was a terrible idea. But she couldn't think of a single one of them right then.

"Well, I'm not going!" she finally announced. "I'll live at Stevie's house, that's what I'll do." Then she buried her face in all three pillows and cried as hard as she could.

"Honey, we'll talk about this in the morning," her mother whispered, clicking off the lamp. "You'll see, it won't be so bad."

In a few minutes, Molly was exhausted. All that crying made her so sleepy. Maybe if she fell asleep she would wake up tomorrow and the worst thing would be that she hadn't finished her ankle bracelet. She would still be having a perfect summer with her friends, just like before.

Her parents tiptoed out of the room. Molly heard her father give a low whistle. Next she heard the sound of Rigg's scratchy nails flying up the stairs. In a flash, his little Toto face was right by her bed.

"Here, boy. Come on up," Molly said with a sniffle.

Riggs was all over her, licking the salty tears away from her cheeks. A jumble of thoughts crowded her mind. Sleepovers at Stevie's and reading scary stories in the dark. The Halloween parade and pizza party at the end of the road. The valentine sticker trading party. Even picturing the car pool fights about who was going to sit in the middle brought on more tears. Molly, Stevie, Laura, and Meg had been friends forever. Now it was all going to end!

"Oh, Riggsy," Molly said, hugging his furry neck as tight as she could. "We can't move to Kansas, we just can't. How can I leave my friends? I can live without food, I can live without water, but I can't live without my friends!"

Riggs snuggled closer, happy to be with Molly. He didn't know this was the worst night of her whole life.

THE COUNTDOWN BEGINS

Molly could barely open her eyes. When she did, they felt all dry and scratchy, so she closed them again. Curling her toes, she hit the corner of the clipboard jammed at the bottom of her bed. She reached down for it, passing four or five crumpled tissues on the way.

She didn't have a cold, and she didn't have the flu. She had something much worse. A feeling that something awful was going to happen.

They were moving. Away from her neighborhood of Crispin Landing. Away from her town of Camden.

She looked around for Riggs, but the spot where he had spent the night was empty and cold. With a long reach of her right foot, Molly knocked down her old stuffed rabbit. He was four Easters old, and his fur was now more gray than white. Still, his whiskered face and button eyes comforted Molly.

He understood her.

"My whole life is ruined," Molly told her old friend, squeezing him so hard that his tattered pink ears flopped forward.

Molly sniffled, then pulled two tissues out of the box by her bed. She dabbed her eyes and aimed the crumpled tissues at the wastebasket. She missed.

As if things weren't bad enough, Molly heard raindrops tapping on the roof. This sound usually made her feel safe and cozy, but not today. Even without getting out of bed, Molly could picture just what kind of day she was going to have — hot and soggy. Everyone crabby in the car pool. Indoor games that all the day campers hated. Baby movies everyone had seen ten times already. Worms in the puddles on her street. Usually Molly loved going to the Mohawk Day Camp, where she and her friends went every

July. But not on the second worst day of her life.

She pulled the sheets over her head. She wasn't going to get out of her bed until her parents came in and told her they had made a big mistake, that they were definitely not moving to Kansas.

Instead, Scotty came in and breathed near Molly's left ear. "Mommy's getting me a big moving van so I can put my guys inside. I'm gonna ride a horse at Grandpa's. Just mine," he announced. "Can you play cave with me, Molly?"

She pulled the sheets tighter.

"Go away! I don't want to play cave."

Molly often enjoyed making a cave out of sheets with her little brother early in the morning. Her mother always made her feel grownup when she, Molly, thought up games that made Scotty giggle.

"Sometimes, you're better than a baby-sitter, Molly." She loved the times her mother said that. Of course, there were plenty of times when she was nothing like a baby-sitter. Like right now, for instance.

"Scotty, Molly's not awake yet," she heard

next as her mother raised the shades at each window. "You go give Riggs his breakfast, and Molly will play cave with you later."

"I will not! I'm going to be busy later," Molly muttered from under the sheets. She was going to play cave by herself, it seemed.

Scotty trotted out of the room making clicking sounds. He was already riding that horse out at Grandpa's.

"I'm not going to camp," Molly announced to her mother. "I hate when it rains and we get all sweaty playing dodge ball inside. I want to stay home!"

"That's just what I was thinking, Molly," her mother agreed, surveying the crumpled tissues scattered by the wastebasket. "It's a good day to be a slug-a-bed. Later, after you straighten up your room, you can decorate the nightshirt you wanted to wear at Stevie's sleepover next weekend."

"And have Scotty get into my paints again?"

Mrs. Quindlen sat down on Molly's bed and gently pulled back the covers. "Scotty is going over to Jason's all day, so he won't get into your things. I have a lot of phone calls to make to real estate agents and movers, but I was thinking we could go to the Yellow Brick Road for egg salad sandwiches later on."

Real estate agents? Movers? Moving wasn't like going to the grocery store or getting the car washed. Her mother was acting as if moving were like Saturday chores. Molly couldn't imagine ever doing one normal thing again like cleaning her room or eating lunch. Didn't her mother realize that?

She had so much to say but all that came out was: "I'm sick of egg salad."

Mrs. Quindlen wasn't about to remind Molly that she once ate egg salad sandwiches for seventeen days in a row.

"Well, it doesn't matter. We'll go to town, and when we get back you can go over to Meg's, the way you girls planned. It's going to clear up by this afternoon."

"We were supposed to go to the pool after camp, remember?" Molly said, as if her mother had ordered the rain on purpose.

Mrs. Quindlen wisely left the room.

Molly looked at her beautiful string bracelet dangling from the clipboard. She didn't care if she never finished the last inch. They probably didn't even have string bracelets in Kansas.

She spent the next fifteen minutes trying to find something to wear. The tag was too itchy on her one clean polo shirt. Her favorite shorts were under the bed, too crumpled to wear. She wouldn't put on her camp shirt because she wasn't going to camp. With a deep sigh, she finally settled on a blue-and-white top with matching shorts.

Molly stood before her dresser. Her mother's old fake jewelry along with some tag-sale treasures were jammed into her jewelry box. On rainy days, she sometimes liked to sort out everything and line up the rings inside the little velvet compartments. But she'd been much too busy to do that lately. Macaroni necklaces, pop-top bracelets, and rings she had made out of faucet washers from the hardware store were all in a jumble.

She separated a tangle of braided bracelets from the heap and put on the special Chinese staircase bracelet that Meg had made her just the other day. Below that she tied on Laura's pink-and-purple wrist bracelet. Pink and purple were her favorite colors.

Now Molly needed something from Stevie.

She rummaged through the box, looking for a lucky lump of greenish rock that Stevie had given her. She stuck it in her pocket. Now she was ready to face the day.

The egg salad at the Yellow Brick Road helped, but only a little. Molly still couldn't figure out how she was going to tell her friends she was moving.

Her mother suggested a few different ways to break the bad news.

"You know, you don't have to tell them at all. I could just mention it to their moms. Then they can tell the girls one by one."

Molly's answer to every one of her mother's ideas was: "I want to tell them myself."

By one o'clock, she was back in front of her dresser, trying on different faces and rehearsing her announcement in front of the mirror.

"You're never going to believe this. The most awful, terrible thing in the world is going to happen," Molly told her reflection, as she made her fake crying face. She noticed some egg salad on her chin and made her scrunched-up face while she removed it. "We're moving!"

Molly's big brown eyes filled up with real tears when she said those words.

Soon there was no more time for her to practice her fake crying face, her surprise face, or her mad face. All the way over to Meg's she just wore her everyday Molly face.

"Did you bring your string?" Meg asked when Molly stepped into the big orange tent in Meg's backyard.

"And your membership card?" Laura giggled. The tent had been the headquarters of five or six different clubs. Two years before, the girls called themselves the Bluebirds, but even Meg, the organizer, couldn't figure out what to do in the club besides look for old bird feathers.

Then there was the Clue Club, which had lasted all of last summer as the girls hid or found clues about people in the neighborhood. Most of the meetings of the Clue Club featured shopping lists and torn envelopes that blew out of people's garbage cans. The end of summer had brought an end to the Clue Club.

No matter how long a club lasted, there were two things they always had — meetings and membership cards.

"I forgot my card," Molly confessed to Laura, the secretary of the current Gypsy Club. "Will you take this instead?" she said, handing over Stevie's green rock.

"Thanks a lot, Molly," Stevie said. "I told you that rock has special powers and should only be used when you really need it."

Molly mumbled, "I really need it," but no one heard her. Meg was busy calling to order the meeting of the Gypsy Club. She banged a small wooden hammer on an old toy workbench. Everyone stopped talking and arranged themselves in a circle.

Molly loved the meetings, whether the girls were supposed to be bluebirds, detectives, or gypsies. She liked the way the tent gave them all orange faces, as if just being in the clubhouse changed the way they looked.

"I call to order the meeting of the Gypsy Club," Meg announced, with a toss of her curly blonde hair. For someone with such blue eyes, two dimples, and pink cheeks, Meg could look and sound awfully official when she began the meetings. Of course, the little hammer and the whistle around her neck helped. "The secretary will take attendance. Laura?"

Laura Ryder tucked her long thick brown hair behind her ears and took a deep breath, but not before two giggles escaped. She sat up straight, smoothed her dark eyebrows, and tried not to giggle again. Like Molly, Laura just loved hiding out in the big tent with her best friends. She forgot everything when she was in there. Her happiness made her giggle, even when she wasn't supposed to.

"Margaret Milano?" she called out.

"Present," Meg answered, as if she were the mayor sitting in the town hall.

"Stephanie Ames?"

"A.W.O.L.," Stevie mumbled as she chewed on a strand of her reddish blonde hair and wrinkled her freckled nose. Sitting still wasn't one of Stevie's strong points.

Laura looked confused. "What does that mean, Stevie?"

"Absent Without Leave," Stevie announced as if that explained everything. But all three of her friends looked confused. Stevie was trying to be funny again, and they didn't always get it.

Stevie sighed. It was no use explaining. She knew things the three other girls couldn't always figure out, like pumping up a tire on a bike, or getting up a tree without skinning yourself, or knowing what A.W.O.L. meant.

Laura spoke up again. "Molly Quindlen? Where were you today, Molly? A.W.O.L. from camp?" she asked, laughing at her own joke. With Stevie and Meg around, Laura didn't often get a chance to say something funny.

"I'll tell you later," Molly said mysteriously. Of course, the girls couldn't wait until later.

"Tell us what? Tell us what?" Stevie wanted to know. She and Molly were the two best friends within the four best friends, just as Laura and Meg were. It was impossible for them to keep a secret from each other for long. All the girls swore they could keep any secret.

It wasn't true.

Laura knew ahead of time about the bike the other girls' parents had chipped in to get for her birthday in May. Meg kept the secret of Molly's getting Riggs last year for exactly one day, when she couldn't hold it in anymore. All the mothers said the girls had radar ears anyway, so it was best not to tell any secrets in the first place. Now Stevie wondered how it was possible for her best, best friend to know something she didn't.

All eyes were on Molly.

"I'll tell you later . . . when I'm ready," she said, not knowing when that would be.

24

Meg looked puzzled, but banged the little hammer to get the meeting going again. "Today, we're going to tell fortunes," she announced. "Look what I brought."

She unwrapped a glass-ball candle holder she had borrowed from the china closet at her house. Carefully, she put the glass ball in the middle of the tent.

"Who wants to go first?"

The girls said nothing. As usual, they let Meg lead the way. She would know what to do.

Meg rubbed the glass ball three times. Then she pushed the button on her tape recorder, and "Horror Sounds of the Night" filled the tent. It seemed this was the way to begin a fortune-telling. The tape was from the Crispin Landing Halloween Party, which was held every year on the corner of the street. Everyone would munch on hot, freshly delivered pizza and listen to "The Monster Mash," then "Horror Sounds of the Night."

Unveiling the ball to the sounds of screams and screeches, Meg said, "Just in case my fortune really comes true, I want to make sure it's what I really want. Ready?" The girls nodded, and Meg turned down the tape recorder. "I see

25

a great future ahead. Lots of fame. Lots of fortune. And lots of fun."

"And lots of rocks underneath this tent," Stevie interrupted, shifting around. She liked being in the tent with the girls for a short time but got restless fast. Everybody giggled until Meg brought them to order.

"Laura, it's your turn," Meg said.

Laura ran her hands over the glass ball three times, the way Meg had done. Her dark, thick hair fell forward as she gazed into the ball. "I see a beautiful forest with me surrounded by birds and deer and baby rabbits."

"Oh, you're going to be Snow White!" Stevie laughed, leaning forward to take her turn at the crystal ball.

Turning up the tape recorder and "Horror Sounds of the Night," Stevie said: "I see . . . I see a great future in the movies." She paused. "Selling popcorn!"

Everyone except Molly dissolved into giggles.

Molly moved up to the ball and stared at it for a long time. Tears came to her eyes, and she wasn't sure she could speak. Finally she said: "I don't have any future. I'm . . . I'm moving away."

The tent was completely quiet. Meg's heart pounded. What would they do without Molly? Laura felt dizzy, as if the tent were floating away. Her own parents sometimes whispered about moving from their rented home someday. What if this gave them the same idea? Stevie's heart was pounding, too. To calm it down, she leaned over her sneakers and twisted the ragged laces.

"Of course you're moving," Stevie cried suddenly. "We're all moving. The earth is moving around the sun, the wind is moving, and your eyes are moving right this minute, Molly!"

"Stevie!" Molly cried. "We're moving away . . . to Kansas . . . for real . . . in August. My grandpa is sick, and we have to go help him with the hardware store. For a whole year!"

"You're just kidding, aren't you, Molly?" Meg said, turning off the tape.

"Yeah," Stevie said. "Stop teasing. You're just trying to get attention."

Laura looked right at Molly. "You *are* just joking. Aren't you, Mol?"

All the girls looked at Molly, waiting for her answer, hardly breathing.

"It's true," Molly said. "We're really going . . . for a year. I hate it. I really hate it."

There was silence in the tent as Meg and Laura and Stevie tried to understand what Molly had said. Then Meg, looking at the tears running down Molly's cheeks said, "At least you're coming back."

"Yeah, it'll be like you're going away to school or camp, or something," Laura said feebly, not believing her own words. "I'm going to miss you so much," she added, knowing *those* words were true.

Stevie kept twisting her laces. She wanted to say how much she would miss Molly, too, but saying it meant Molly was really going. Molly couldn't go, she just couldn't. It was all a joke. "I can't believe you're going to Kansas. They have tornadoes there! You might wake up one day and find yourself in Oz!"

"No, *this* is Oz," whispered Laura. "She's going to wake up and find herself in Kansas."

THE ALMOST VERY
LAST SLEEPOVER

Summer afternoons were the busiest times in Crispin Landing. People drove through the roads slowly, avoiding the kids who were out jumping rope, skateboarding, or just sprawling on the curb, taking a break from the hot fun of playing. When they got home from work, parents stopped to toss balls or Frisbees to their children.

Molly was glad her dad was on his summer schedule, just teaching a couple of hours of history in the morning. He could play ball or Frisbee with Molly and Scotty half the day, and often did. And she found it very useful to have him around to help her do things, like carrying half her belongings to Stevie's for an important sleepover.

"They should call these things wakeovers, not sleepovers," Mr. Quindlen told Molly as he walked her down to Stevie's house, just two doors away. "We should have taken the car," he teased, carrying a sleeping bag and a tote bag in one arm, while trying to balance a large cardboard box in the other.

"Oh, Daddy," Molly sighed. Her dad always made the same old jokes. He called McDonald's Happy Meals "Unhappy Meals." He sometimes called Friendly's "Unfriendly's." And he always called sleepovers "wakeovers," because the girls stayed up half the night and were always crabby the next day. "This might be my very last sleepover," Molly protested.

Mr. Quindlen raised his eyebrows. "I have a feeling it won't be the *very* last," he said with a smile.

In the week since her parents broke the bad news about moving to Kansas, Molly kept talking about the very last this and the very last that. The Very Last Fourth of July Picnic. The

Very Last Trip to the Mall. Even the Very Last Visit to the Dentist!

This sleepover, probably not the Very Last One, began with a phone call from Meg giving a list of instructions on what to bring. "Glitter nail polish, your string kit, your Barbies, the nightshirt you made, your sticker book. Oh, and 'The Big Toe,' of course." The girls couldn't possibly have a sleepover without Stevie's reading of that story. No matter how many times they heard it, they always shrieked when she got to the line: "Where's my to-o-o-o-e?" Even on this hot July afternoon, Molly got the shivers just thinking about it.

"Looks like you'll be gone a week, Mol. Don't forget to come home some time in the near future," Mr. Quindlen told her when they reached Stevie's.

Molly sighed again. "Oh, Daddy." He always teased her about bringing too much stuff. "I *need* everything I brought."

"You *need* this?" Mr. Quindlen asked, raising one eyebrow, as he held up a computer-paper box that had all sorts of things sliding around inside it. What seemed like an ordinary computer-paper box to Mr. Quindlen was a potential "cozy hotel" to Molly and her friends. The girls no longer remembered how they came up with the idea of "cozy hotels." All they knew was that they liked transforming old boxes into cabins, attics, apartments, or houses where they imagined themselves living together someday. Without their parents, of course. Setting up cozy hotels was one of the main purposes for having a sleepover. Everyone but Mr. Quindlen knew that.

Molly rolled her eyes. "Meg said to bring it, that's all."

"We-e-ell, if Meg said to, then I guess you need it," Mr. Quindlen teased as he kissed her forehead. " 'Night Molly. Don't stay up too late. Remember you — "

"I know, Daddy, I know. You don't have to tell me again." Every time there was a sleepover, all the parents made the girls promise not to stay up too late and not to be in bad moods the next day. They always promised, but it never worked. They just had too much to do and talk about, and they didn't mind being crabby the day after.

Molly rang Stevie's doorbell. Usually she walked right into the Ameses' house whenever she wanted. But today she was early.

Besides needing that old computer-paper box, Molly needed to talk to her best friend. Stevie had been acting pretty odd for the whole week since Molly told her about moving to Kansas. All the other girls took turns crying or listening to Molly cry, but not Stevie. It was a lot easier for Stevie to make a goal in soccer or a home run in softball than to tell her best friend how awful she felt. Joking about tornadoes and Kansas helped Stevie pass the time until she would be able to say, "I'm going to miss you."

The sound of television coming from the Ameses' den drowned out the doorbell, so Molly walked into the house and set down her things. There was always plenty of TV at Stevie's, and not just children's programs like at her house.

"Oh, hi," mumbled Mike, one of Stevie's older brothers, who was passing through the living room.

"Hi," Molly mumbled back. Stevie was the only one of the girls who had older brothers. Molly wasn't used to being around older boys close up like that. Sometimes Dave, who was thirteen, and Mike, who was eleven, teased the girls by skateboarding or biking within an inch of where they were standing. Or else they made

33

weird noises at them in the dark. Mostly, though, Stevie's brothers acted as if their sister's friends were no more alive than chairs or tables.

"Molly, you're here," Mrs. Ames said, coming in the door with a couple of grocery bags. "Here, grab this one. There's a big bag of M&M's near the top. Dig in if you like."

Molly lifted the bag from Mrs. Ames's arms. Sure enough, it was filled with goodies, including a family-sized container of Cheez Balls, Molly's favorite. She knew they might not get dinner on time at Stevie's, or any dinner at all, but there would still be plenty to eat.

"Mike? Dave? Go out to the car," Mrs. Ames called out to her sons. "I've got a trunk full of groceries to put away!"

Molly reached down into the bag for the promised M&M's but couldn't bring herself to take any. At her house, treats came at snack time, not around the clock like at Stevie's.

"Go ahead, Molly. Help yourself," Mrs. Ames said, tearing off the top of the bag. "If you don't get it now, everyone else in this house will beat you to it! And where is my starving daughter, by the way?"

Molly shrugged. She had no idea where Stevie

was. Obviously no one else did, either. That was another great thing about Stevie's house. Everybody came and went when they wanted, and Molly felt a little older when she was over there. Since Stevie's parents were divorced, there just weren't as many grown-ups around to keep an eye on the snack cabinet. When they were in charge, Dave and Mike didn't care whether Stevie and her friends brushed their teeth or watched too much television. And Mrs. Ames was happy just having Stevie's friends over.

"Well, she'll show up, probably just as soon as we get these groceries put away. Here, Molly, see if you can unload this bag for me while the boys bring in the rest," Mrs. Ames told her.

Molly knew her way around the Ameses' kitchen. Plenty of times she and Stevie would open every single cabinet and the refrigerator, then study what was inside. The results of their surveys were crazy sandwiches like peanut butter and bananas, or mayonnaise and strawberry jam on crackers.

Mrs. Ames was right. Just after everyone finished shelving all the groceries, Stevie burst into the kitchen, hopscotching over the black and white tiles on the floor.

"What did you buy, Mom? I'm starving!" In a flash, Stevie had popped open the top of the Cheez Balls. One by one she tossed them in the air and tried to catch them into her open mouth.

Nine Cheez Balls later she said hello to Molly.

"How come you're so early? Meg and Laura aren't coming 'til six-thirty. Let's go outside."

The girls went to the side of the house. Stevie grabbed one of her brothers' basketballs and bounced it around the driveway.

"Stevie, do you think everybody will forget me when I'm in Kansas?" Molly asked her friend.

"One more try," Stevie said, aiming the ball toward a net that was way too high for her.

"Stevie! Do you think everyone — " Molly began.

"Well, a year's not that long. Especially in Oz. A year in Oz is like three months anyplace else," Stevie answered, aiming the ball just the way her brothers had taught her.

She missed the basket, then missed again. Stevie didn't often miss like this, but every time Molly started in about moving, Stevie got very un-Stevie-like. She missed a basket or wobbled on her bike until she thought of a wisecrack to lighten things up again. It was a bad habit, she knew, like chewing on her hair or biting her nails. But she couldn't help it.

"Just think, now you don't have to worry about getting Mrs. Higgle next year like the rest of us." Mrs. Higgle was one of the fourth-grade teachers, and all the kids were afraid of her, from the lunchroom. When she sat at a table she forced kids to use a fork for everything. Even French fries!

"I'd rather get Mrs. Higgle than go to Kansas," Molly said.

"Maybe we can trade places. Dave and Mike had her, and she hates our whole family. Remember how she caught Mike with the firecrackers that time? I'm in big trouble if I get in her class."

"They might have somebody worse in Kansas," Molly said. She wanted to get back on the subject. Was Stevie going to miss her or not? Or was she just going to keep shooting baskets as if Molly weren't there. "I don't want to move. I'm going to miss everything. The Christmas party, the play, the Valentine's Day party, even Halloween." Molly knew she was going to miss a lot more than that. She would even miss the broken-down wooden glider she was sitting on in Stevie's yard. And the swing hanging from the maple tree. She would miss every leaf, every blade of grass, every —

"I'm sure they still have Halloween in Kansas. You can go as Dorothy," Stevie said, racing around the driveway as if a big basketball game were going on. She just wasn't one to sit around missing things like Valentine's Day parties that were a million years away. Molly was here right now, and Stevie just wanted to do things with her, not talk about what they wouldn't be doing when Molly was gone.

"Want to ride bikes?" Stevie said next.

Molly didn't really want to ride bikes. She wanted to sit around and mope a little more. She wanted her best friend to cry her head off because she was moving.

"Okay," she sighed. "I'll get my bike out of the garage."

For the next half hour, the girls raced up and down the street, aiming their bikes straight for the puddle that always formed in the circle at the end of Half Moon Lane. Pretty soon, the girls had a line of dirt up their backs from all the puddles they hit. Stevie did wheelies and always skidded her bike to a stop just a heart-stopping second before she reached the fire hydrant, or a tree, or the curb.

"Stevie! Stevie!" Molly shrieked every time Stevie's bike streaked by just inches away. She was so careful herself, putting on her brakes way before she needed to. She made slow, wide turns, not hairpin ones like Stevie. Still, she loved having a daredevil for a friend. While the wind blew her straight, brown bangs away from her face, Molly smiled her big two-teeth-missing grin.

Kansas was a million miles away.

"Should we go get our bikes, too?" Laura asked Stevie when she and Meg got to Half Moon Lane at six-thirty. They definitely looked like gypsies with all the stuff they were carrying. Sleeping bags, backpacks, doll carrying cases, boxes, and pillows. Both girls looked as if they were going on a month-long vacation.

"We're not going to have time to ride bikes," Meg announced. As usual, she was in charge of the plans, and they didn't include bikes.

"Good," Laura said, relieved. She was still a little shaky on her bike. She loved looking at her new two-wheeler, but riding it made her a bit nervous. She was very careful around things like bikes and swing sets and roller skates. What didn't make her the least bit nervous was ballet, where her feet mostly touched the ground. She and Molly had been taking lessons at Miss Humphrey's since they were three.

Stevie, on the other hand, always needed something to climb, pedal, or roll on, like a skateboard or a bike. Meg was somewhere in the middle. She loved gymnastics and seemed to spend half her time hanging upside down from her swing set or showing the other girls how she could race across the bars three at a time.

"Let's go set up," Meg said, putting an end to the bike talk.

Up in Stevie's room, the girls cleared space for their four sleeping bags. They shoved soccer shoes, a hockey stick, some comic books, and at least six pairs of dirty socks into Stevie's closet.

"Should we pick numbers?" Meg asked. To avoid arguments about who slept where, the girls usually wrote their names on four slips of paper, then arranged the sleeping bags in that order.

"Let's do it the way we did last time," Molly suggested.

The girls then set up. This meant arranging their sleeping bags in a straight row, Stevie's next to Molly's and Meg's bag next to Laura's. In no time, Stevie's room looked like a Girl Scout cabin ready for inspection. Except for the closet, of course. The girls' mothers could never understand how the girls could be so orderly when they set up their things like this and so very messy when it came to socks and underwear.

"I'll go get us some food," Stevie announced, growing a bit impatient with the endless smoothing of pillows.

The girls were soon in heaven. Tonight was the night Meg wanted to find out how she would look with straight hair. While Stevie fetched the snacks, Laura ran off to the bathroom to get Meg's hairbrush as wet as possible.

"You're so lucky, Molly. You already have straight hair," Meg sighed, admiring Molly's perfectly smooth hair.

"I know, but it doesn't do me any good. My mom says I can't grow it any longer unless I stop screaming when she brushes it, but I can't help it!"

"I know, I know." Meg sighed. "My mom wishes I could be bald sometimes."

"I can't picture you bald, Meg." Stevie laughed when she walked into the room with a tray of snacks. On a hot summer night like this, Meg's curly hair was wilder than ever. "You just need your coat sheared once in a while."

"She does not, Stevie," Laura declared, walking into the room with a dripping hairbrush and a jar of pink goo.

The girls spent the next ten minutes trying to flatten Meg's hair, but as soon as sections of it dried, one or two curls popped up again.

As they often did, the girls found dozens of things to do. Stevie wasn't about to have anyone flatten her scraggly hair, but she was glad to play cat's cradle with Molly while the girls talked about how disappointed Jennifer, their day camp counselor, was that morning when Dave, the swimming instructor, didn't show up for the third time that week.

"I can't believe he's got chicken pox," Stevie cried. "I'd be embarrassed at his age," she added, making Dave sound as if he were fifty instead of seventeen or so. "I mean, gross. All those spots like a little kid. Ugh!"

"He probably caught it from one of the campers," Meg pointed out. She loved Jennifer, their counselor, and because Dave was Jennifer's boyfriend, Meg had to defend him, spots and all.

"I'll never get to be a Shark if he doesn't come back soon," Molly said, lifting off an intricate cradle of strings from Stevie's fingers. The Sharks got extra free swim and could go on the high dive at the day camp pool.

"I'll teach you," Stevie said. "That airplane exercise for the breaststroke, it's a cinch. I'll turn you into a Shark by the end of summer, I promise."

"I won't be here at the end of summer, remember?" Molly said, getting her pinkie in a tangle. She bunched up the cat's cradle and threw it down on her sleeping bag.

Of course Stevie remembered. She was only trying to make Molly feel better. She just didn't know how, that's all.

"I can't believe you're really going in a month," Laura said softly.

"Three weeks!" Molly cried. "Twenty days if you don't count today."

Stevie brightened. "Let's count today 'cause we're going to stay up all night. That'll make it longer. We should have sleepovers every night. That way we'll see you twice as much," she added, pleased with her idea.

"Fat chance of that, Stevie," Meg interrupted. "You know how our parents are about sleepovers."

Molly and Laura groaned. "We know, we know."

"We have to figure out some way to keep Molly here," Meg said, squinting her blue eyes tight as if that would somehow keep Molly from leaving. "There's got to be something we can do."

Molly had hoped she could get through one single day without crying. But now it looked as if she was going to have a perfect record. "I don't want to go," she wailed. "I just don't want to go. Every morning I wake up and wish it weren't true. But everything, even the food I eat, reminds me I'm leaving in just a few weeks."

"Guilty food, I bet," Meg said knowingly. "When I had to go to the hospital, my mom let me have ice cream whenever I wanted. Then when I was better, we went back to the same old rules."

"Dave and Mike said that when my dad

moved out, they got lots of presents," Stevie added. "I wish I was old enough to remember."

Meg looked over at Molly and could see that all the presents in the world, or even ice cream for breakfast, weren't going to help Molly right now. "She doesn't want presents, guys, or special dinners. Molly just wants to be here with us," Meg reminded everyone.

Molly sniffled. "Thanks. I feel a little better." She paused. "And a little worse."

"Worse? How come?" Stevie asked.

"Better 'cause you guys are the best and dearest friends ever. And worse because there won't be anyone else like you out in Kansas."

The girls had tears in their eyes, but they were smiling a little, too. They liked the idea that in a huge state like Kansas there weren't going to be the close, wonderful friends as there were right there in the tiny state of Rhode Island.

"If only you could live here, Mol," Stevie said.

Of course, the girls had discussed this idea endlessly with their parents. At least seventy-two times in the last week. They just couldn't see why Molly *had* to go with her parents. All of them could easily imagine having Molly right in their houses, just like a real sister. First at

Stevie's, then at Meg's, then at Laura's house. It was a great idea. Unfortunately their parents didn't think so.

"My mom says we can write to each other," Molly muttered to her sleeping bag.

Stevie wrinkled her nose, and Laura turned down her bottom lip. Writing was too much like homework.

"Why are you looking like that, Meg?" Stevie asked. "Did you swallow something down the wrong pipe?"

Meg's blue eyes were shining like glass, and her face was pinker than usual. "You guys. Don't you get it? We can be with Molly, and she can be with us."

Molly sat up, the first one to catch on to what Meg was thinking. "A club! Is that what you mean, Meg?"

"A brand-new club. The best we ever had!" Meg cried. "We'll be pen pals."

"I could set up a post office at my house with a box and office supplies and stuff," Meg began.

Molly felt a glow come over her. What a great idea! Having a club that she could belong to in Kansas would keep her part of the group even when she was far away.

"We'll write a letter every single week you're gone." Laura took a deep breath. "Maybe we can even do a round robin like my mom told me about in a magazine. You put stuff in the envelope like stickers, pictures, and sayings or poems — "

Meg continued Laura's thought. "Yeah, then the next person reads what's in the envelope and adds her own stuff. We could even do tapes and codes and stuff."

Stevie was watching Molly the whole time the other girls were talking. It was just like Meg to cook up something like a pen pals club, but Stevie wasn't sure where she fit in. She hated writing. Her handwriting was a mess. She had trouble writing to her own father down in North Carolina. She couldn't picture herself writing to Molly. She just wanted to *be* with Molly.

"What about you, Stevie?" Molly wanted to know. "Are you going to be in the club?"

"Sure," Stevie answered. "But pen pals is a dumb name for us. We're more than pen pals, we're *friends*. Friends forever!"

"Stevie is right," Meg said. "We are friends and that's what we'll be — the Friends Forever Club."

"Great," Laura said. "I love it."

For the first time, Stevie felt like crying just the way Meg and Laura had. Writing letters meant Molly was really going away. Then she looked at Molly's expectant face and got an idea of her own. "Hey, remember that catalog we had last year when we were trying to get money for the trip to Boston?"

The girls nodded. Every family in Crispin Landing had ordered something from the catalog to help the third-graders raise money. Customers had bought wrapping paper, personalized pencils, and dinosaur notepads.

"We could get special stationery," Stevie said with excitement.

Molly hugged Stevie. "You're so great for thinking of that. It'll be so much fun picking designs. Then we'll be a real club and real friends even when I'm far away in Kansas."

"We can sign our name, 'Friends 4-Ever,' " Meg added, already picturing how nice that would look above her name.

The four friends, not yet far away, immediately forgot about all the things they had planned to do all night. For once, they even forgot about reading "The Big Toe." Instead they stayed up

48

until midnight discussing plans for their letter-writing club and how wonderful it would be to send mail to each other.

And they weren't the least bit crabby the next day, either.

BIG PLANS

"Stevie, you're dripping on the catalog," Molly said, smoothing her towel.

"Sor-ree," Stevie answered, squeezing water from her strings of hair right onto the catalog again.

Molly, Stevie, Meg, and Laura had set up an island of their beach towels on the warm cement deck of the Camden town pool. After swimming, the girls liked to spread out in the sun and work on their string bracelets, or their sticker books, or do nothing at all. Today, though, they were studying the novelty catalog of stationery items

Stevie had dug out of her mom's magazine pile. Ever since the sleepover two days before, the almost-pen pals had been discussing designs every spare minute, even at the pool.

"I'm definitely getting the unicorns," Laura announced. She pushed her sunglasses to the top of her head so she could see the pages better. "Definitely." She had been going back and forth between the balloon stationery and the unicorn stationery almost every day. "Is everybody watching, 'cause I'm writing it down. In pen. That way I can't change my mind." Laura pressed down hard on the pen and filled out the form. "There!"

"Well, I still can't make up my mind," Meg sighed. "There are three different kinds of cat stationery, but none of them looks like Marmalade."

"They couldn't get Marmalade's picture on one sheet of paper," Stevie joked.

Marmalade was only two, but she was already on a diet. Meg had begged her parents for a pet ever since she was three years old. For the longest time her parents made all kinds of excuses why she couldn't have one. Then, when Scotty Quindlen's allergies started up, the pediatrician

51

told the Quindlens that Marmalade had to go. He went to Meg's.

"I guess I have too much cat stuff already," Meg said with a sigh. "But these are so-o-o cute."

Then Molly studied the catalog. This was an important decision. "I kind of like this one with the ballet slippers." She looked a little sad and far away for a second. "But they might not have ballet in Kansas." Talking with her friends about the stationery and their new club was so much fun. What bothered her was the reason for the club.

She needed stationery because she was moving away.

Right away Laura noticed Molly was upset. "Look, Molly, there's rainbow stationery. You're so good in art and — "

"And you'll be living on the other side of the rainbow," Stevie finished.

"It's perfect," Meg said.

Molly knew her friends were right. She loved rainbows, real ones and pictures of them.

"Okay, that's what I'm getting," she said softly, taking the catalog from Meg's towel, then filling out her section.

Stevie noticed how quiet Molly seemed to be getting. "Hey, we're official now, Mol. Or at least we will be if you can help me pick something out."

With a totally straight face, Meg said, "Gee, Stevie, I didn't think you'd need stationery since you'll be using invisible ink."

"Ha, ha, ha," Stevie answered. "Well, you're wrong. I'll be using *visible* ink, so there!" Stevie didn't want Molly to think she wouldn't be writing as much as the other girls. The whole subject of being a pen pal instead of a plain old friend still upset her, and she didn't want anyone to make jokes about it.

"Molly, now can you help me pick something out?" Stevie asked her friend.

"How about these fluffy chicks and duckies?" Meg said in a squeaky baby voice, which she knew drove Stevie up a wall.

"Never mind Meg, Stevie. I know the perfect thing for you," Molly said, pulling the catalog from Meg's towel. She flipped through it several times until she found just what she wanted. "Take a look," she told Stevie.

"These little pink storks?" Stevie asked. She wrinkled all eleven freckles on her face.

53

"No, silly," Molly sighed. "These."

Stevie looked where Molly was pointing. Her best friend had picked the best design — a row of bright blue high tops very much like Stevie's real-life lucky sneakers. "You're right, it's perfect for me," Stevie said. She beamed at Molly. Maybe this writing stuff wasn't going to be so hard after all. "Now can I go in the water?" she asked her friends.

"Dismissed!" Meg cried, and in a flash Stevie was in the pool.

"You really did find the perfect Stevie stationery," Laura said.

"Yeah, now all we need to do is find an automatic pen that will write for her," Meg said.

"Meg!" Laura cried. "Molly's worried enough about Stevie writing."

Molly nodded.

"I'm sorry, Molly," Meg said, immediately ashamed of her remark. "Really I am. I feel so awful about your going that sometimes I just make jokes so I don't have to think about it."

"We all do, Mol, especially Stevie," Laura said. "Otherwise, we'd be crying all the time."

"Thanks for saying that, guys. I guess that's

why Stevie keeps making all those Kansas jokes and kidding around about all our clubs. Do you think she'll really write? Do you? She doesn't even write to her father that much." Molly was sure if her own parents were divorced and one of them was far away, she would write every day.

Laura moved closer to Molly's towel. "Don't worry, Molly. I'll help Stevie. Maybe she can dictate her letters, and I'll write down the words. Don't forget the round robin idea, either. If Stevie gets stuck, maybe she can send you things — you know, pictures or things she collects, and stuff."

All three girls shrieked: " 'N' Stuff!" 'N' Stuff was what they called all the things they collected. 'N' Stuff might be seed pods, marbles, pretty rocks or shells, stickers, braided bracelets they made, or plastic prizes from the Talking Parrot machine at the children's shoe store in town. The important thing about 'N' Stuff was that it couldn't cost much and definitely couldn't be thrown out. It was settled. The girls would send Molly lots of 'N' Stuff.

"Thanks, Laura. You guys are the best friends

in the whole world," Molly answered. She felt nice and warm now, the way she always did when they sat by the pool after a cold swim.

Meg and Laura took off their sunglasses and Molly led the way to the water slide.

"Last one in buys me a snack!" Molly cried.

The girls stayed in the water until they were as wrinkled as raisins. Even then they didn't look up when Mrs. Ryder showed up at the edge of the pool.

"Girls, time to go home! Time to go home!" she repeated. No one heard her over the shouts, the shrieks, and the splashing. When Laura finally came up for air after doing a cannonball off the low dive, Mrs. Ryder was waiting for her by the side of the pool.

"No shoes on the deck, Mom. Pool rule," Laura said, sounding just like one of the lifeguards.

"And no daughters in the pool," Mrs. Ryder said right back. "You girls were supposed to be all ready at five-fifteen."

"We're ready, we're ready," Laura answered, barely paying any attention to her mother. In fact, Stevie, Meg, and Molly were still in the water and hadn't checked the huge pool clock, either. It clearly said five-fifteen.

"One more jump, Mom. Please. Just one more," Laura begged.

Mrs. Ryder sighed. "Okay. Just one more," she agreed. She knew her daughter would probably squeeze in three more cannonballs if she could. She smiled at Laura, pleased to watch her in the water. Mrs. Ryder didn't care much for the water and had never really learned to swim. She was proud of Laura, who loved swimming and who had even been the first of the four girls to pass the Camden town pool's deep-water test two years before. Laura was so considerate she never bragged about it. The other girls had been happy for her and only a tiny bit jealous. Of course, they made sure to pass their own deep-water tests the very next day.

A half hour later the girls were finally dressed and ready to go. They gathered up their damp things and trudged out of the dressing room, their plastic flip-flops slapping against the wet cement floor. Molly noticed the sign first, right behind the desk where she picked up her pool pass. There it was, jumping out at her, a sign that said, FAMILY FUN DAY, AUGUST 9TH.

"Hey, guys, you realize you can be on the watermelon relay this year?" Pam, one of the junior lifeguards, asked.

"We know, we know," Meg muttered, realizing right away that one of their group was not going to be pushing a watermelon across the pool with her nose on August 9th. "Sorry, Molly. I saw the sign when I came in. I was hoping you wouldn't notice it."

"Never mind, it doesn't matter," Molly said, turning her head away from the bulletin board. She swallowed hard, remembering all the Family Fun Days they had always shared, when even their parents did silly things like go down the water slide or jump in the pool all dressed up. On August 9th, Molly would be thousands of miles away from all that.

The pool parking lot was hot and dusty, and Molly felt that way, too. Mrs. Ryder's car was an oven, so Molly's back and legs stuck to the hot vinyl seats. Now she was tired. When she was tired she wanted her mother. And when she wanted her mother, she got mad at herself.

"Maybe you can come over for dinner," Stevie whispered to Molly, hoping to cheer up her friend.

Since Molly was so tired, she almost hoped her mother would say no. Still, a tiny part of her wanted to be with her best friend every single second, now that there weren't very many seconds left until she moved to Kansas.

"First stop, girls," Mrs. Ryder cried out a few minutes later. "Got all your things, Molly?"

Mrs. Quindlen ran out to the car to meet Molly. Riggs somehow managed to hop onto the backseat and started jumping all over the girls and licking them.

"Riggs, come out here this second!" Mrs. Quindlen ordered. "I don't know what's gotten into this dog. Today, he got away, and I didn't catch him until Church Street. Is this everything?" she said, picking up Molly's soggy towel and beach bag.

"Mom, can I have dinner at Stevie's? Please, can I?" Molly begged. Now she definitely wanted to go to Stevie's more than anything. She forgot all about taking a bath to wash off the sticky chlorine. She forgot about her cool cotton nightgown and finishing *Caddie Woodlawn* in bed.

Mrs. Quindlen frowned. Molly knew that face could mean two things. Her mother was too tired to put up a fight, or else her mother was too tired to let her break a rule.

"Molly, I told you, you're supposed to check with me before you start making plans like this." Mrs. Quindlen broke a rule of her own, which was not to scold Molly in front of other people.

Molly's eyes felt itchy, and her ears were pounding. Still, she wasn't going to cry.

Mrs. Quindlen was still frowning. "I'm sorry, Molly, you're tired, I think you should come home."

Well, Molly certainly didn't need her mother to tell her that. "You never let me do anything!" she cried, right before bursting into huge sobs. Mrs. Quindlen didn't bother to point out that Molly had either been visiting at different homes or having friends over every day for the past two weeks. Not that Molly would have heard any of this. She was crying and shaking too hard.

"You'd better take the other girls home, Lynn," Mrs. Quindlen said to Laura's mother. "This is a no-win situation," she added in a whisper.

Molly hated when her mother said that. A no-win situation always meant her mother won and she lost. Now she knew she wouldn't be able to go to Stevie's for dinner even if there wasn't a crust of bread in her own house.

When the car finally pulled away, Molly felt as limp as an old balloon. Mrs. Quindlen put her arms around Molly, who couldn't resist crying into her mother's crisp cotton sundress. They stood on the lawn like that until Molly's loud sobs turned into quiet little hiccups, and they went inside.

"Let's go in, Molly. Maybe we can read together in your bedroom before dinner. You can show me how far you are in *Caddie Woodlawn*. By the way, we're having your favorite for dinner tonight. Grilled hamburgers."

THE GOOD-BYE GIFTS

"Ten, nine, four, two, one, three, sixteen. Here I come!" Scotty shouted. Molly scrunched herself as small as she could inside the cardboard box she was supposed to be packing.

"Are you in there?" Scotty yelled, banging on the flaps, then looking inside. Molly had buried herself under some old stuffed animals and doll blankets, so Scotty moved on to the next box.

"Oh, no! I thought you two were packing, not dawdling," Mrs. Quindlen cried when she saw the state of Molly's room. Messy. Even from down inside the box, Molly recognized Mrs. Quindlen's voice as the very one she had used a few weeks before when she found Molly's wet bathing suit lying on the cherry coffee table.

"Come out of there this second, Molly Melinda Quindlen!" her mother said, lifting the box lids to get a better look at her daughter.

Molly looked up with one eye. Hovering over the edge of the box, her mother's face seemed huge.

"The movers are coming tomorrow for the boxes going to Kansas. Everything else, *everything*, Molly, is going to the warehouse at the end of the week."

As far as Molly was concerned the end of the week was the end of the world. If dawdling would keep that from happening, then dawdling was what she was going to do.

"Everything, Mom?" Molly heard Scotty ask. Her mother moved away from the box, thank goodness, which gave Molly a chance to climb out without looking silly.

"Molly and me packed, see?" Scotty said, pointing down into one box that had exactly three small cars in it. He was doing his five-year-

63

old best to block his mother's view of a battered toy garage he and Molly had rescued from the trash pile.

Molly wanted to kiss Scotty right then. He was having a hard time, too, she realized, when she saw him clutching an old airplane.

Since Molly was older, she knew the next few words were meant just for her.

"There is still a lot of packing to do, and you really have to get going, Molly," her mother said in a shaky voice. Molly knew that voice, too, since her mother usually used it right before a big explosion.

"But, Mom, I tried, I really tried," Molly wailed. "How am I supposed to know what I *have* to have in Kansas?"

Her mother shifted voices. "You wanted to do it all, remember, Molly? And you haven't really started."

This was true, Molly admitted to herself, kicking a rubber ball straight into the corner. Every time she thought about the rest of her things sitting in a big, dark, cold warehouse for a whole year, she stopped packing and started playing instead. How did they expect her to fit eight years' worth of toys into two boxes anyway? It wasn't fair.

"I did so start. Look at all my stuffed animals. They're right here." Molly pointed to a half filled box.

Her mother sighed. "You have to choose! You just can't send all that. Now why is this in the box?" her mother wanted to know. She held up a yellowed dog with patchy fur. "He doesn't even have a name. He shouldn't be going to Kansas."

"He does too have a name. It's . . . it's . . . Snowball," Molly stated, pleased that the old stuffed dog she had bought from Stevie at the neighborhood tag sale for twenty-five cents now had a name. Maybe having a name meant he could go to Kansas.

Mrs. Quindlen was not smiling the way Molly hoped she would. "Molly, these are the boxes we are sending ahead. The packers are picking them up tomorrow. Daddy and I will pack your things if you can't decide what is staying and what is going into storage."

"I can too decide. Snowball is definitely going."

"I'll help you, Molly," Scotty said, standing next to his sister. He stuffed a ratty pink blanket into the box. "See?"

"Scotty, you come with me. I need a helper in the kitchen for a big job," Mrs. Quindlen said. "Molly has to work by herself for now."

Molly sniffed. Then she sniffled. She was the one who usually helped her mother with the big jobs. All Scotty would do was make a mess.

"Mol-ly," her mother warned.

One hour later, Molly still had only half a box packed, and her room was still one big mess. Packing made her so grumpy. She wished she hadn't taken on such an awful job. If only her mother would quit telling people how Molly was so grown-up she wanted to pack her own things. What Molly wanted was a real grown-up to tell her what she was going to need.

Molly heard a special knock. She tapped back, giving the signal that the coast was clear.

"Surprise!" Stevie cried.

"We came to help you out," Meg said. "I brought my clipboard, and we'll help you make a list."

Mrs. Quindlen stood in the doorway with half

a smile on her face. "The girls promised to help you pack in one hour. After the job is done, we're all going to La Piazza for pizza-no-sausage-no-peppers."

"I'll get it done this time, Mom, promise," Molly said, full of new energy for the job.

Meg was beaming under her blonde curls. While there wasn't enough time to turn this job into some kind of club, she had a few ideas.

"First you have to get in uniform, Molly," Meg said.

Molly noticed the three girls had on their red Mohawk Day Camp shirts and their beanies. Stevie's was on backwards, of course. Meg was also wearing a silver whistle around her neck, probably to keep her workers on the job.

While Molly scrambled into her camp shirt, Meg announced the plans. "My mom gave me this checklist from a book she has about moving. Everybody should have a special job, and everything you pack should go on a list on the outside of the box."

Except for Stevie, who was trying to shoot a foam Nerf ball into Molly's wastebasket, the other girls nodded in agreement.

"Your mom said there are only two boxes you can send," Meg said. She was so relieved she wasn't the one moving away.

"That's all?" Laura and Stevie cried out in disbelief. Neither girl could possibly imagine getting her whole life's worth of things into just a couple of boxes.

"It's easy," Meg explained, trying to keep up team spirit. "One box will be for 'N' Stuff and cozy hotel things. Laura and I can get that one ready. This one will be for everything else. You and Stevie can do that one." Before they knew it, Meg had labeled each box with a fat black marker, and the girls got busy sorting everything into the boxes.

Molly felt better already. Her friends knew just what to do. Of course, they did the job with a lot of sighing over Molly's old things, which they all remembered playing with over the years.

"Ooo, here's your Billy doll," Laura said, cradling a small one-armed rubber baby doll. At one time, all the girls had Billy dolls and they probably still did. Somewhere.

Stevie had never been much for Billy dolls, but she knew just what to do with the few scarred blocks lying around. She got busy constructing a perfect little cabin until Meg stood over her, clipboard in hand.

"Stevie, we've only got one hour! Maybe you should check with Molly's mom about those in case she wants Scotty to have them."

"Hey, you just gave me a great idea!" Stevie cried. "How about this, Molly? If there's anything you want to bring but it doesn't fit in these boxes, say it's for Scotty."

"Great idea, Stevie," Molly said. In no time she and her friends had a pile of things they were going to convince Scotty he had to have. Once again, her friends came to the rescue with another super scheme.

"Meg, what are you doing with my shoe box?" Molly asked when she saw Meg toss an important box into a big black trash bag. "I might need that."

"Your grandpa's store will probably have loads of neat boxes, don't you think? " Meg said.

"Yeah! I didn't think of that," Molly said. Having her friends help her out like this made the terrible packing job a lot easier.

Even with all the oohing and aahing and re-membering and playing, the girls managed to get most everything packed until the boxes were bursting.

In the middle of everything, Riggs came flying into the room, looking for trouble.

"Riggs! Get out of here," Molly yelled when he snatched a small stuffed chick and wouldn't give it up. "Where's your Buddy Bear, Riggs?" When the Quindlens adopted Riggs, he chewed every stuffed animal he could find. Molly had the great idea of getting him his own stuffed animal, which everyone called his Buddy Bear. The plan worked. Until recently Riggs pretty much played with Buddy and left Scotty's and Molly's things alone. But for some reason he'd started going after their toys again in the last few weeks.

"Is this it?" Meg said, holding up something that might have been a stuffed bear at one time. Now it looked like some sort of eyeless creature with flattened, kind of mossy, fur.

Molly grabbed the thing and tossed it out in the hall. "Go get it, Riggs!" she said, as Buddy flew through the air. They had enough trouble without her dog chewing and chasing her things. "My parents said dogs and cats sometimes get upset when people are moving and stuff is all over the place. Riggs has been bad lately. He chewed my mom's new leather sandals and ate a hole right through the mattress on their bed."

"Marmalade goes crazy when he sees our suitcases packed," Meg, the cat expert, said.

"Sometimes animals know more than people do," Laura agreed. She didn't have a pet yet, but she'd read a lot about them so that she'd be ready when she did get one.

Mrs. Quindlen stuck her head in the door and looked over the room. "You've all done a great job. Looks like you only have a few things to go. See you in about twenty minutes."

"Okay, Mrs. Quindlen," Meg said.

The girls sat in a circle staring at the few leftover toys. These were things all of them had played with once but not anymore — some faded collectible animal figures, a scarred soccer ball, and a few tattered dress-up clothes.

There was no more room in the boxes for anything else.

All the girls were thinking the same thing: How awful it was to stick everything in storage cartons for a whole year. It didn't matter that some of these toys had been lying for ages under

Molly's bed or in the corner of her closet or in back of her dresser. Each one was a precious memory, and the girls couldn't bear to finish the job.

"Maybe my mom will let me keep some of your stuff at my house," Laura suggested. She wanted so badly to help Molly part with her special things. Keeping something of Molly's would be like keeping part of Molly, too. Laura swallowed hard and held her breath so she wouldn't cry.

"Wait a minute!" Molly said suddenly. "Meg, give me your clipboard and pencil. You guys go wait outside the door until I call you."

The girls looked totally confused. How could Molly be so excited when they were so miserable? What was she going to do?

"C'mon. I've got to do this fast," Molly said. "It'll only take a few minutes."

Molly shut her bedroom door and began sorting through the toys. Then she scribbled on three pieces of paper. She was ready.

"I'm done! You can come back in," she said to her friends, who were huddled in front of the bedroom door, still looking puzzled.

"Okay. Sit down everyone," Molly directed.

"First, I need complete silence. I just wrote out my will. Now I'm going to read what I'm leaving to each one of you."

Unable to resist a wisecrack, Stevie joked, "I thought you were moving, Molly, not dying."

"This is a different kind of will, Stevie, so just listen, okay? Ready?"

The three girls nodded.

"To Laura Ryder, I leave my silver tiara, even though it isn't silver anymore and it's kind of smooshed. I want you to have it because it will remind you of the wonderful times we had in ballet together.

"To Meg, I leave some of the plastic figures I collected. You'll know just how to sort them out and display them so they look bright and shiny again.

"To Stevie, I leave my old soccer ball, even though it doesn't have much air left in it. You were the one who made me like soccer even when I didn't want to!"

Molly smiled at her three friends. "I feel much better. I know you guys will take good care of my things. Now they won't have to sit in dark boxes while I'm gone."

"Thanks, Molly," Laura said quietly. "I'll put

the tiara with my hair ribbons and remember you every time I go into that drawer."

"And I know just where to display these," Meg said, surveying the rubber ponies that once had bright flowing tails, and the small plastic animals that only needed a good scrubbing. Meg was so proud her friend trusted her with her collection.

"Thanks for the soccer ball, Mol," Stevie said, kicking it softly around Molly's nearly bare room. "I'm going to find the leak and patch this up. It was lucky once, and maybe it'll be lucky again."

"I'm the one who's lucky having such good friends," Molly said, smiling. "Now c'mon. I'm starving. Let's go get pizza!"

RUNAWAY RIGGS

Molly swayed in the hammock, her two legs dangling off each side like crooked branches. In the last days before the Quindlens were to move, everyone tried to make sure she was so busy she wouldn't think about it. But even with all the errands to be run, trips to the pool, and special dinners at her friends' houses, each day there seemed to be a stretch of time no one could fill up.

These were the times Molly went out to the backyard and swung slowly in the faded striped hammock, thinking of everything she was going to miss. The hammock for one thing. Its strings were unraveling from all the times she and her friends played mummy in it. It was so old, her parents weren't even packing it.

She looked up in the locust tree, loving each of its feathery leaves. Looking at the tree from this position, it was hard to believe everyone always called it The Junk Tree, because it shed constantly and sent up horrible roots the barefooted children always stubbed their toes against. Molly would miss this tree, terrible roots and all.

She looked at the sturdy birdhouse she and her dad had built, still nailed tight to the tree. Each of the last three summers, Molly and her father had gently removed the small sparrows' nests inside. They always hoped that more colorful birds like chickadees or finches would visit, but somehow sparrows seemed the right sort of bird for The Junk Tree. Molly stretched a leg and kicked the tree root she knew was right under the hammock. Even the sparrows would be here next week, but she would not.

When she felt this way, she didn't seem to have a bone in her body. Her legs and arms went limp as she lay in the shapeless hammock, knowing that there wasn't a single thing she could do to stop Saturday from coming.

She pulled both sides of the hammock over her head like a cocoon. Maybe she could change into something else, a different girl whose parents didn't have this terrible plan to move away.

Suddenly she was rocking back and forth, as if a hurricane had blown in. Hurricane Stevie.

"Hey, it's time for the meeting, Mol. I came by to get you." Stevie pulled apart the edges of the hammock and made her googly face at Molly.

Molly laughed. Then she straightened up and brushed off tiny leaves that were already twirling down to the ground, as if The Junk Tree had pushed ahead its leaf-shedding schedule just for Molly's sake.

"I'm ready." She got out of the tippy hammock, then called through the screen door, "Mom I'm going to Meg's."

"Fine, okay," her mother called back. The sound of her voice bounced over the walls of the nearly empty rooms.

"Isn't it weird how your parents keep saying 'Fine, okay' to everything this week? I mean, what if you said, 'Hey, Mom, I'm taking the keys and going for a drive.' 'Fine, okay.' Or, 'Hey,

Dad, I'll be home at midnight.' 'Fine, okay.' "

Molly and Stevie giggled at the thought. "I wish I could just say, 'Hey, Mom, I'm moving into Stevie's house.' If only they would say 'Fine, okay' to that!"

"If only," Stevie agreed.

The girls took the long way to Meg's so they could check on who was out on the road on this late July afternoon. Stevie hopped on one leg practically all the way to Meg's, and Molly walked a tightrope on the curb, careful not to lose her balance.

"Hurry up, you two," they heard Meg yell from her bedroom window. "I've got a surprise."

The girls let themselves in and dashed upstairs. What had Meg cooked up now?

"What took you guys so long?" Laura and Meg both cried at the same time.

"Come over here," Meg said, leading the girls to her bed. "Ta-dah!" She whisked a blanket off four boxes of stationery lined up on the bed.

"Ooo," Laura cried as she ran her finger over the border of the unicorn stationery.

"Neat," Stevie said. She took the top sheet from her box and turned it into a paper airplane.

"See? My letters won't need any postage."

The girls all laughed.

"How do you like yours?" Meg asked Molly.

Molly couldn't say a word at first. How couldn't she help liking the pale blue paper with a border of rainbows at the top?

"It's perfect," she breathed, stroking the box.

Stevie said proudly, "We even paid extra to get double the amount."

"You can still use the paper when you get back next year," Laura pointed out.

"If you have any left," Meg added. "I mean, we'll be writing so much. You'll see. I worked out a schedule and everything. Now isn't anybody going to say anything about my room?"

The girls looked around. Meg had turned her room into her idea of a post office. Her desk was covered with trays, a paper-clip holder, rubber stamps, a rainbow of markers and pens, stickers, colored tape, construction paper, and even a bright red stapler. Meg's parents both worked at home, so she always had the neatest office supplies. Now it was all arranged under a big poster that said, FRIENDS 4-EVER POST OFFICE.

"See, every week at our meeting we'll put our letters in this box," Meg announced after Laura took attendance, "and I'll make sure they're stamped. We'll send one out every other day. That'll be three letters a week for you, Molly."

Molly was thrilled and miserable at the same time. In less than one week, she would have letters, not friends.

As usual, Meg was all caught up in her plans. She wanted every detail of the club to be just right. "I wish, wish, wish Ed, the mailman, would let me have that leather mailbag from his cart. It would be perfect instead of this," she sighed. She held up an ordinary carton, which she had tried to decorate as a mailbox. Meg just couldn't give up the idea of getting Ed's mailbag. The girls still remembered when Ed used to let them push the cart from house to house as he delivered the mail. Ages ago, of course, when they were little. Now they needed that bag for important things like their club.

"Maybe we can make Ed an honorary member," Stevie suggested. "I mean, he's going to be delivering all our letters."

Molly bit her lip. "Not *all* our letters. Some strange person in Kansas is going to be delivering mine."

"Oh, Molly," Meg began. "I'm sorry. I wanted all this to make you feel better."

"We spent our allowances and birthday money on the stationery," Stevie said, sitting down on the bed next to Molly. "I got it instead of a new lacrosse stick."

Molly laughed and cried at the thought of Stevie giving up something having to do with sports for something having to do with writing.

"I *am* happy about the Friends 4-Ever Club, really," Molly said. "It's just that I — "

"We know," Laura interrupted. "You just want to stay here."

Meg looked worried. "Does the club make you feel worse, Mol? 'Cause we don't have to do it, or at least we don't have to talk about it today."

Molly got up and hugged Meg. "I love the club, really I do. Tell me the plans."

Meg began slowly, careful not to get carried away as she sometimes did. "Well, I marked all the days we're supposed to write to you." She held up a kitten calendar and flipped to the month of August, which featured an adorable orange tabby. "Starting on August third, I'll write every Monday. Laura will write on Wednesdays, and Stevie will write on Saturdays. How's that sound?"

"It sounds like homework, Meg," Stevie said.

"Stevie!" Meg cried.

"Saturdays are okay," Stevie mumbled, correcting herself. Now why did she always have to put her big sneaker foot in her mouth? she wondered. Molly was feeling bad enough already.

They felt terrible all over again when they noticed M's MOVING DAY marked in big red letters on the August-first part of Meg's calendar.

Laura noticed right away that Molly's eyes were filling with tears again. "My mom said I could call you sometimes, Molly. At night, when it doesn't cost too much." She patted Molly's hand. Laura loved her new stationery and seeing unicorns printed on it. But it wasn't going to take the place of having the real, live Molly right there.

Moving was so awful.

Stevie was getting uncomfortable, so she made another airplane and another typical Stevie joke: "Air mail. Get it?"

The girls laughed but only a little. Everything they did this week, even talking about their letter writing club, was part happy, part sad. They were happy that their parents were letting them have even more fun times together like extra dinners and sleepovers. But when the girls got tired or quiet, they also got sad thinking about the reason for all the extra fun.

Molly would be gone in just three days.

Even Meg could see that being Friends 4-Ever could only help them feel a little better about Molly moving. It couldn't keep her from moving. She got busy looking for the big manila envelopes she'd made for each of the girls. Maybe that would cheer them up.

"Here's where you can keep your stationery at home," she said, handing the envelopes to each of her friends. "Look inside."

"Hey, neat," Laura cried when she discovered that Meg had tucked some postage stamps, stickers, and a pencil with rainbow lead inside each envelope.

"Is the meeting over?" Molly wanted to know. "I mean, now that we have our stationery . . ."

"I guess so," Meg answered. For once, she didn't know what to do next. The stationery they had talked about so much and saved for was here, and so was Molly. The club couldn't really

83

get underway until Molly moved and they had someone to write to. The thought of that made all the girls quieter than they had been all day.

"See you tomorrow," the girls said, turning to wave to Meg from downstairs.

Outside, three long, droopy shadows crept down Doubletree Court. No one was hopping on one foot or skipping over cracks.

Laura stopped at the curb in front of her house. She wanted to give Molly a big hug. Instead she just said, "I know we'll be great pen pals, Molly. I promise."

Molly hugged her box of stationery close to her.

"I'll write, too, Molly," Stevie told Molly when they got to her house. "You might have to get a translator to read my handwriting, though. See you later."

Molly planned to put her stationery box right into her going-to-Kansas suitcase, where it wouldn't get lost. Her desk and her dresser had already been sent off to the storage warehouse.

"Mom, Scotty? I'm home," Molly shouted when she got inside her house. She hated the way her voice echoed in the rooms. The movers had already come to get most of the furniture.

They would come for the rest Friday afternoon, and the Quindlens would spend that night at a nearby motel with a pool and special buffet breakfast.

Molly didn't care about the pool or the breakfast. She just wanted her own things back.

"I'm home," she cried again, but only her voice answered back. Molly hardly ever came home to an empty house, and she didn't like it. Where were her mother and Scotty anyway?

"Riggs? Come here, Riggsy." she called out. No Riggs. Maybe they were all out walking.

Molly checked the backyard, but no one was there, either. She heard the phone ring, then ring some more. She ran in and picked it up. "Hello, who is this?" she asked.

"Molly. Good, you're home. It's Mommy. Riggs got away again, and I'm calling from a phone on Warburton Avenue."

Molly's big brown eyes opened in alarm. Warburton Avenue was blocks and blocks away. Worse, it was the busiest street in town. All the trucks whizzed through there. How would they ever notice a little gray dog like Riggs?

"Can I come there, too, Mom?" Molly asked.

"No, you stay put. I've got the car, and I'll be

right home. Just keep an eye out for Riggs on our street until I get there, okay?"

"Mom, what if he's really, really lost this time?" Molly cried.

"We'll find him, don't worry, Molly. I'll be right home."

Molly ran outside and scrambled up the swing set. That gave her a view of several nearby yards. But there was no Riggs dodging in and out of bushes and fences and no little dog terrifying the neighborhood squirrels.

She was scared, almost as scared as the time she got on an elevator and the doors had closed before her mother had a chance to get in. She'd thought she was never going to see her mother again. What if she never saw Riggs again?

Molly thought about all the lost dogs she had seen in the movies or read about in books. Dogs like Benji and Lassie, who found their way home because their owners didn't go moving away to Kansas. Molly knew Laura Ingalls Wilder's dog, Jack, had come back to the family's covered wagon, but he only had to cross a prairie, not Warburton Avenue.

Molly heard her mother's van pull into the driveway.

"Did you find him? Did you, Mom?" Molly cried, running to her mother.

"Not yet, honey, but we will, don't worry."

"We can get a puppy in Kansas. And a pony," Scotty told his sister.

"I don't want a puppy or a pony!" Molly shrieked. "I just want Riggs." Oh, how she hated it when Scotty, who was only five, was so reasonable while she was crying her head off!

Molly ran up to her room, too miserable to go searching for her dog. She wasn't going to leave it until Riggs came home. She wasn't going to eat until Riggs was sitting at her feet, waiting for her to drop crumbs under the table. Of course, they didn't even have a table anymore, either! Everything, except their suitcases, beds, a few boxes, and a fuzzy black-and-white television, was in storage or on its way out to Kansas. Molly sobbed into her pillow, which her parents were going to allow her to bring on the trip out in the van. Just one pillow.

It was their fault. Didn't everybody know how upset Riggs must have been when he saw his favorite sleeping chair go out the door and into a big moving van? Didn't anybody realize how awful Riggs must have felt when they packed up his old rubber hot dog and the wicker basket he slept in? Animals were just like people. They had feelings, too, but nobody ever thought about Riggs and how upset he might be.

Molly flipped her pillow over when it got wet and soggy. She felt wet and soggy, too. And hungry. But she wasn't going to eat, not while poor Riggs was roaming around the streets and alleys of Camden, hungry and miserable, too.

MOLLY'S ALMOST LAST GOOD-BYE

"Judy, can I send Molly and Scotty over? Bill and I are going to ride around some more. Honestly, I can't believe that dog picked today to get lost, what with everything else we have to do in the next couple of days!"

Molly wasn't supposed to eavesdrop, so she couldn't point out to her mother that Riggs hadn't gotten lost on purpose. All anyone thought about was packing and getting ready, when poor Riggs might be hurt or upset.

Mrs. Quindlen noticed Molly standing outside the kitchen. "I'm sorry, Molly, I didn't mean to sound so annoyed at Riggs." She sighed. "I guess I'm just mad at me. I've been so busy running around, I wasn't careful about keeping the door latched. I should have known better. Riggs probably wanted to get away from all this upset." Mrs. Quindlen looked around the half empty house in dismay. She couldn't seem to find a pencil or a pair of scissors, let alone their poor dog.

"Why do I have to go to Stevie's?" Molly wanted so much to be in the car when they found Riggs. She could already feel his little sandpaper tongue licking her in happiness. She could wrap him in a blanket and feed him bits of ham and dog treats when they got home.

Molly felt her father's arm around her shoulder. "We need you and Scotty to stay around here in case Riggs comes back while we're out in the car. The more people we have looking, the sooner we'll find Riggs."

"What if we don't find him, Daddy?" Scotty asked what Molly didn't dare say out loud. Her brother had gotten himself all dressed up in cowboy boots and a fire hat to go out looking for Riggs. But his trembling chin gave away his feelings. He and Molly were both terrified they would never see their dog again.

Mrs. Quindlen bent down and peeked under Scotty's hat. "We'll find him. We're not going to stop looking until we do."

"Really, Mom?" said Molly. She needed to know that Riggs, not moving, was the number one thing they had to do.

"Really," Mrs. Quindlen answered. "Now you two head over to the Ameses. Judy's gotten all the kids organized so that we don't just wander around in the — "

Mr. Quindlen interrupted before she could say "dark." No one wanted to think about that. "Here's a flashlight for each of you."

Molly's heart was pounding. She remembered once when Riggs was just a puppy and had run in front of a car on Crispin Landing Road. The screech was terrible and so were the seconds before the Quindlens finally caught him, running in and out of the Ryders' daffodils as if nothing had happened.

They had to get out there fast. "Okay, Scotty. Let's get our equipment," Molly began. "We'll need a couple of leashes, some dog treats, a whistle, a blanket, and these flashlights."

They packed Scotty's red wagon with everything they might need and headed down the street. The street lamps hadn't come on yet, but it was starting to get dark. Molly tried not to think about Riggs being gone all night.

"Hi, Mol," Mrs. Ames said when the search party arrived. "I've got a couple of sandwiches ready if you want to take them along while you go out looking. Your mom said you didn't have time to eat. How about it?"

"No, thank you," Molly answered. Her stomach was churning too much to eat.

"Me, neither," Scotty said, still looking worried. If Molly wasn't eating, he wasn't, either.

The front screen door screeched open, and Stevie, Meg, and Laura burst into the Ameses' living room. "Oh, Molly, it's so awful!" Meg cried. The three girls surrounded their friend. "We'll help you find Riggs! Stevie has a good plan."

Stevie was flushed and completely out of breath from running around trying to help Molly before it was too late. "Okay, guys, here's what I did. I got out the old Clue Club map that we made of all the houses and roads in the Landing."

Stevie pulled out a large creased map the girls had spent hours working on the year before, when they were studying maps in school. Mrs. Kirk, who was the best teacher in the whole world, had given the girls special permission to work on a group map. It had come in handy plenty of times when the Clue Club needed to solve neighborhood mysteries. Maybe it would help them find Riggs.

"Here's what I thought," Stevie began. "We only have a little time before it gets dark, so we have to split up. I divided the Landing into three parts. My brothers and Scotty will cover the Lower Landing. Laura and Meg are going to search Doubletree Court and Heritage Road." Stevie looked at Molly. "We're going to search Half Moon and Sunridge Terrace."

Molly gave Stevie a hug. "Thanks, Stevie. I can't think straight. I need somebody to tell me what to do."

Meg and Laura came up to Molly, too.

"We did something else, Mol, as soon as we found out about Riggs. We put up this poster all over the neighborhood. My dad's out right now putting them around town. See?" Meg said, holding a flyer that said: LOST DOG. There in the middle of the sheet was a blurry but unmistakable picture of Riggs.

"He looks a little smudgy, but you can still tell it's Riggs," Laura said.

"See? It's got all our phone numbers on it," Stevie pointed out. "That way somebody's sure to answer the phone."

"Thanks," Molly said quietly. "This makes it a little easier."

"And easier to find Riggs," Meg added.

Dave and Mike came up from the basement with ropes and flashlights. "C'mon, Stevie. Are we gonna look for this dog for real or on your map? I know every yard in the dark," Dave Ames said casually.

This was true. He and his brother and sometimes Stevie popped out of dark shadows or even became dark shadows when they streaked by on their skateboards with their friends. Meg, Molly, and Laura often watched them zigzagging under the street lamps long after the girls had to be indoors.

Molly felt better knowing Stevie's brothers

would be out there hunting for Riggs. They would know every little corner where a dog might go.

"Bring Scotty back here and find me if you go down to the bridge," Molly said shyly. She had a feeling that Dave and Mike would be going to the footbridge that connected Crispin Landing with the next neighborhood over. The girls were strictly forbidden to go there without a grown-up, but they never quite knew why. They thought it had something to do with beer cans and cigarettes. The Quindlens often took Riggs for walks there during the day, when the stream and footbridge looked kind of pretty. At night-time, though, it seemed like a big dark hole with mysterious noises. The thought of it gave Molly the shivers, and she didn't want Scotty going there, even with Dave and Mike.

Everyone gathered up flashlights, whistles, and ropes. Molly handed each member of the search party a plastic bag of Riggs's favorite dog food. Just in case.

"Let's all be back at eight o'clock," Stevie said. She hadn't noticed that no one except Meg was wearing a watch.

In no time, they had scattered to their territories. Stevie and Molly went up to each house and put a Lost Dog flyer in the mailboxes. Except for Mr. Melham, who hated children, most of the neighbors were happy to let the girls search through their bushes and yards.

Usually Molly loved her neighborhood at this time of year, at this time of the evening, when it was almost the hour to end the day's playing, but not quite. Usually she loved the warm summer scent of climbing roses at Mrs. Plumley's, who had the prettiest garden. She liked listening to the cozy sound of silverware clinking in the kitchens of some of the houses. She even liked the way her heart practically pounded itself right out of her chest, when she and her friends would sometimes spot a skunk poking around some of the yards.

Tonight, though, there were no hide-and-seek games, no playful solving of mysteries. This terrible search was for real, and with each empty yard, Molly felt worse and worse. In house after house, no one had seen Riggs today. The movement of leaves was the wind, not her precious pet, and the small animal that darted under one of the street lamps was a fat white cat, not a little gray dog.

"Riggs, Riggs, where are you?" Molly called, but no Riggs answered back.

Finally, Stevie and Molly ran out of yards to check, so they headed back to Stevie's, the leashes dangling loosely.

"You go in, Stevie. I want to wait out here for a few more minutes. Just in case," Molly said, knowing that there would have been a crowd of people out if anyone else had found her dog.

Stevie banged the screen door. "No luck. How did you do?"

Molly moved away from the murmuring voices and light coming from Stevie's house. She retraced her steps and went back to yards she had just visited. No Riggs.

"Here boy, here boy," she called as she re-checked under two parked cars and a few bushes where Riggs might have chased a cat. All the bushes were catless and dogless.

"It's no use," she sighed, winding Riggs's red leather leash tight around her hand.

Molly went back to Stevie's house. Everyone had returned, dogless, too. Molly felt hot and itchy. The mosquitoes had been biting. Now that the search was over, she felt every single bite and scratched until she drew blood.

"I'm sorry, Molly," Laura said. "We thought we saw him in the Bashers' backyard, but it was Mr. Hall's dog."

"Hey, we're not giving up, team," Stevie said firmly. "Tonight, leave your outside lights on and put food in a bowl by the door. Each person take some of the dog food, some flyers, a rope or leash, and we'll meet at Meg's tent first thing tomorrow morning. Now I'm going to see if Mom will start the grill and cook some hamburgers. Riggs might smell it and come back here."

This was a great idea, Molly thought, but she was too tired and hopeless to say so. How could she stop looking for Riggs when it meant he would have to spend the night outside? How would she ever fall asleep without knowing he was safe at home?

An hour after going to bed, Molly was still wide awake. Her parents had told her over and over that they would surely find Riggs the next day. It would be light out. People all over town would see the posters. But in the late silvery light of the moon, Molly didn't believe a word of it. Riggs was gone, and soon she would be gone, too.

She kept getting up to go to the window, just in case Riggs found the huge bowl of food she had left near the back door. But no, the only movement was the locust tree swaying in the summer wind.

Molly noticed her stationery lying right on top of the suitcase where she had left it. Maybe Riggs had the right idea, Molly thought. Maybe running away was easier than moving away.

Molly thought about a poem her mother used to read to her:

I'll go away and never come back.
  Rickety-rack
  I'll never come back.
I'll put my clothes in a paper sack.
  Rickety-rack
  In a paper sack.

Away I'll go and never be seen.
  Stickety-lean
  And never be seen.
And they'll be sorry they were so mean.
  Stickety-lean
  That they were so mean.

Molly kept thinking about that poem. Riggs had been upset enough to run away. She was just as upset about leaving everything she knew. She would go and look for Riggs herself. No matter how long it took, she just had to find him. Everyone could just go to Kansas without her.

Her suitcase and two duffel bags were already packed with her things. Molly grabbed the top sheet of paper from her new box of stationery. She dug through her small bag of office supplies and pulled out her rainbow pencil. She began writing.

Dear Friends,

I can't go to Kansas until I find Riggs. He won't know where we are if we leave without him. He's all mixed up about moving, that's why he ran away. I know he needs me. I know he's calling for me. I have to find him.

My mom and dad will still have Scotty.

He wants to go to Kansas. He'll get a new puppy and get to ride a pony. After a while he won't even miss me.

I know you'll take good care of the toys I gave you. I'm sorry I won't be in Kansas to get your letters. The pen pals club was the best club we ever had. And you're the best, best friends I ever had. I'm going to miss you so much.

I hope you won't forget about me. I won't forget about you.

Your Friend 4-Ever,

Molly

Molly looked over her letter. She knew just where she could put it so that her friends would see it first thing in the morning. She got out of bed and put on her flip-flops. She grabbed the letter and the big black flashlight her dad had given her.

She didn't worry about waking her parents. Twice now, her mom had fallen asleep wearing her daytime clothes. All the packing made everyone so tired. And upset.

Tiptoeing through the house, Molly opened

the sliding door in the back. The yard was silvery and bright from the full moon. She had no trouble slipping through the bushes that separated her yard and Mrs. Plumley's. From there, she cut over to Meg's backyard, where the orange tent seemed to be breathing in and out in the warm night breeze. Molly unzipped the screening and stuck her letter inside where her friends couldn't miss it the next morning.

By then, she would be hours away. If she could just find Riggs. She took a slightly longer way back to her house. Maybe, just maybe, he was nearby. She peeked into the O'Connors' yard next door, but nothing moved except a scary-looking white nightgown hanging on the clothesline. Mrs. Plumley's yard was silent, too. Even the birds and squirrels she fed during the day were sound asleep now.

Though it was a warm night, Molly shivered in her thin summer nightgown. Was Riggs shivering, too, afraid and alone on this same night? Tomorrow was pickup day. Maybe he would come around and knock over cans the way he sometimes did when he was bad.

"Please, please let me find him," Molly whispered to the darkness as she made her way to the front of her house.

There were large rubber and metal garbage cans lined up at the foot of each driveway on her road. But no dog had knocked down a single one of them. Molly stood there with her arms folded to stop the shivers. How strange to be out so late all alone. For a second she remembered how she, Meg, and Laura believed, really believed, that there was a witch's face inside the oval glass street lamp, a witch that would scoop them up if they walked in the circle of light the lamp shed on the road.

Now she was afraid, but not because of lamps that looked like witches. Molly was afraid because her dog was never coming back. He never wanted to go to Kansas and this was his way of telling the family.

Molly hugged herself closer, feeling her ribs through the thin cotton gown. She felt like just another shadow on the road. No, Riggs wasn't coming back tonight. It was no use looking. The garbage cans were safe. No little part-Schnauzer was going to knock them over tonight. Tomorrow, she would run away just as soon as it was light and try to find him then.

Molly crept back toward her house. She pictured her friends crying and upset when they realized she was missing. She imagined her parents driving up and down the streets looking for her. Maybe they would put up a poster of her right next to the one for Riggs. Maybe her picture would be in the newspaper.

Molly was so lost in her thoughts, at first she didn't hear the panting behind her. Then she felt something brush against her leg. Fur. She jumped with fright. Looking down, she saw a pair of shiny eyes looking up at her. Riggs's eyes.

"Riggsy, Riggsy, you came back!"

She picked him up. He licked her cheeks, her eyelids, her ears. He made funny, whimpering little sounds, then happy, grateful sounds.

Molly opened the sliding door expecting Riggs to fly in. When he didn't, she turned around. Riggs was busy eating up the dog food Molly had put in his special bowl on the back steps. How hungry he was!

"Oh, Riggsy. You're back, you're back."

Molly realized she was back, too, back home.

Riggs looked up at Molly, happy that she was there. Then he put his nose back into his bowl.

"I guess home is where your bowl is," she whispered. "Even if it's in Kansas."

FRIENDS 4-EVER

"Good-bye, little houses. Good-bye, room," Molly whispered to her walls.

Her bed was gone. Her ballet poster was gone. The calendar opened to August the first was now gone, too.

Her mother called up the stairs. "Come on, Molly. You're supposed to be at Meg's in a few minutes."

Molly touched one of the pink houses on the wallpaper, the one she had once imagined had a mouse family living in it.

"Good-bye, Mouse Family."

She heard her father's footsteps echo in the empty hallway.

"Saying good-bye, Molly?"

Molly knew she would cry if she said even one word. Instead she let her father pick her up, all sixty-three pounds, and she cried into his Red Sox T-shirt.

"Let's go downstairs, Molly Melinda," he whispered.

When her dad put her down, Molly dabbed her wet red eyes with the hem of his shirt. "One more minute, Daddy. I just thought of something."

"Okay, just one."

Molly reached into her backpack and took out the rainbow pencil Meg had given her. She walked into her closet, and on the inside of the door frame she scribbled a message. Then she skipped to Scotty's and her parents' room and did the same thing. Each time she wrote a special message in tiny letters in some hidden part of the room.

"I'm ready," Molly announced when she got back downstairs. "We can go."

Now her mother was the one crying into her dad's Red Sox T-shirt.

"Don't cry, Mom." Scotty comforted her. "The moving guys said they'll bring our chairs back. And my toys."

Molly, her mother, and her father laughed, then hugged each other in the middle of their empty living room while Scotty galloped around and around them as if he were already on a pony in Kansas.

Mrs. Quindlen slowly pulled away and dried her eyes. "I guess I'm ready. We'll drop you off at Meg's for your last club meeting while we get settled at the motel." She checked her watch. "I guess we'll come for you around five, then we'll have dinner at the restaurant. Maybe a swim, too."

The Quindlens got into their van, which was packed to the roof with suitcases, pillows, travel games, and two thousand miles' worth of snacks for the trip to Kansas the next day. They clicked their seat belts on without anyone reminding Molly that, yes, she still needed one even though they were only going around the block. And Molly, for a change, forgot to ask why Riggs didn't have to wear one. Everyone stared straight ahead, too upset to look back at their house on Half Moon Lane.

Molly felt fluttery and strange when they pulled up to Meg's. This was going to be the last real club meeting she would attend for at least a year. She wanted to fly from the van. And she wanted to sit there forever.

"We're here, honey," Mr. Quindlen said as Molly sat there, still buckled into her seat belt.

"See you later," Molly finally mumbled. She opened the door, and when she did, Meg's mother, Diane Milano, was standing there.

"I know we've said good-bye a million times already, but I was hoping you could all come in for a little bit," Mrs. Milano said to the Quindlens.

Molly was puzzled. What would her family do at a club meeting?

The Quindlens piled out of the van and went up to the door. Everything was so quiet. Molly knew her friends just had to be there. After all, this was her very last day.

"Meg, Meg, I'm here," she shouted upstairs.

Suddenly heads popped up from behind chairs, tables, couches, and doors.

"Surprise! Surprise!" voices shouted from every corner.

Molly's feet were glued to the floor. Ed, the

mailman, was there looking very different without his blue uniform. The Melhams were there, too, though Mr. Melham looked as if he wanted to be back at home working on his lawn and chasing dogs and kids away. Mrs. Plumley was there in a white dress with small pink flowers. Half the neighborhood seemed to be crammed into the Milanos' living room.

Molly and her parents couldn't seem to close their mouths. "This is the End-of-Summer party," Mrs. Milano announced.

Now Mrs. Quindlen was crying all over again. "How did you do all this? I can't believe it. I just can't believe it."

Molly curled her toes into her sandals. She loved the annual party the neighborhood always held to say good-bye to summer. It usually took place on her street. But now she could see people streaming up Doubletree Court with folding aluminum chairs and bowls and trays of food. When Molly looked closer, she noticed Big Tom and Little Tom Basher setting up the grill between the two trees that gave the street its name.

"Are you surprised?" the girls asked Molly.

She was much too surprised to answer.

Soon, the party was underway. Once the

grown-ups got talking they forgot all about the kids, who were busy chasing each other in and out of the yards. The girls, of course, had their meeting all planned, and the party just added to the fun. Now they had piles of food to eat, which they brought out to the clubhouse tent.

"I can't believe you're going to eat three of those," Laura said to Meg, when she came into the tent with a huge plate of food that didn't have one healthy thing on it.

"Well, the hot dogs were too black, and the hamburgers were too red," Meg answered, as if that explained why she had three frosted brownies on her paper plate.

"Mmmm. These are so good," Molly said. She was munching a still-warm macaroon that Mrs. Plumley had made. Her fourth one. "This is so great. It's just so great."

"What's not so great is this tent," Stevie said. "We're going to have to throw it away after today." She had just dripped mustard on the floor of the clubhouse, and her macaroni salad was about to join it.

"You guys. I can't believe you guys kept this a secret," Molly told her friends.

"Our moms kept the secret," Meg admitted.

"My mom's the Landing President this year, and she got the idea of having the picnic early so everyone could come. She set up a phone tree like the one we have at school, and your family was the only one that wasn't on the list."

"Yeah, then our parents threatened to kill us if we even breathed a word to you," Stevie said. "See, we're still alive."

"We didn't want to have to say good-bye to you at the motel," Laura added.

"This is much nicer," Molly said quietly. All week long she had tried to picture her last day with her friends. She knew there would be a lot of laughing and a lot of crying. But she had a hard time imagining all this happening in a tiny motel room.

Now Molly was exactly where she wanted to be.

Stevie coughed, then jabbed Meg with her elbow. "Meg, aren't we going to start the meeting?"

That was odd, Molly thought. Usually Stevie acted as if having an official club meeting were more trouble than going to the dentist.

Meg got out her little hammer and pounding

bench. "I call the meeting of the Friends 4-Ever Club to order. First order of business, Laura?"

"There's just one thing today," Laura said. She got up and went out of the tent for a second. When she came back inside, she was holding a giant box wrapped in rainbow paper. Laura handed Molly the present. "It's from all of us."

Molly was almost afraid to open the box. The sooner she opened it, the sooner today would be over.

"C'mon, silly," Stevie urged. "It's not going to explode. Don't worry. I didn't put the rubber snake inside this time. Promise."

Stevie never could resist putting joke items into birthday presents. Sometimes they were rubber bugs, sometimes real ones. The girls usually opened a Stevie present from as far away as possible.

Molly pulled off the purple yarn and stuck it in her pocket. Stevie reached over and ripped off the paper. "C'mon, c'mon," she said.

When Molly lifted the lid, she saw a small leather photo book inside. Four faces grinned back at her, the faces of the four pen pals. Of course, when the photo had been taken on the last day of school, they hadn't been pen pals yet, just four friends hugging and making silly faces for Mrs. Milano's camera.

"It's a memory book," Laura said.

"My mom went through all our albums and picked out pictures of the things we like to do together," Meg added. "See, there's even a couple of pictures of when we were babies."

Molly touched the first picture. Yes, there they were, the future pen pals in diapers. There was even a photo of them without diapers! Molly flipped through the memory book and saw the great times they had had. There were the girls standing next to their two-wheelers. In one snowy picture, the girls were having a picnic in Meg's backyard. The memory book had pictures of so many birthdays they had shared, even the one where just the four of them showed up because they all had chicken pox together.

"Oh, neat!" Molly cried when she got to the last picture. In it, Stevie, Meg, and Laura were crowded into the photo. They were holding a sign that said: FRIENDS 4-EVER.

Molly closed the book. "Thanks guys, this is so neat. I'll keep it right by my bed and look at it every night."

"Hey, that's not all. Look in the rest of the box," Stevie ordered.

Molly pulled apart the tissue paper and found a folded T-shirt inside. She spread it out on the floor of the tent and saw the three smiling faces of her best friends imprinted on it. Holding it up against herself, she said, "Now you'll always be close to my heart."

"And your stomach and your back," Stevie added. "Now c'mon, open the rest of the stuff."

The box was filled with things to make her laugh and cry and always remember her best friends. There was a piece of broken pavement, which Stevie explained was from Half Moon Lane. Meg's father had framed the famous Clue Club map so Molly wouldn't forget where everything was. And Laura had painted a picture of Molly's house.

Finally, at the bottom of the carton was a shoe box pasted with pictures and scrawled with messages. On the lid, in rainbow print, was the word LETTERS.

"Oh, you guys are too much," Molly said, carefully lifting the lid.

"We tried out the stationery before you came over," Meg said.

115

"To see if it worked," Stevie laughed.

Molly's heart was pounding. She had a feeling she was going to cry any minute. She unfolded the first letter and saw Laura's unicorns and her very first letter to Molly:

Dear Molly,

I can't stop thinking about all our great times. Remember the ballet recital when Miss Humphrey let us be the only princesses, but my foot got caught in my costume? You saved my life in front of all those people by dancing extra until I got untangled.

Now when we do warm-ups at dance class, all I'll see is an empty space in the mirror where you should be.

Guess what? I'm crying again. Here's a big splash:

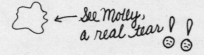

See Molly, a real tear!

I promise to think of you a lot. Especially when I walk through leaves or see the moon or look at my ballet slippers. I feel awful and you're not even gone yet!

Your Friend 4-Ever,

Laura

P.S. *We'll miss you.*

"The next one's mine," Meg said, when Molly reached into the letter box again. "See, we wrote these right before you came over so we'd have letters to start off the club."

Molly unfolded Meg's letter and smiled at the gray kittens tumbling at the edge of the paper.

Dear Molly,
Thank goodness for the Friends 4-Ever Club. Every night after you told us you were

moving (boo-hoo) I couldn't sleep. How could we do anything without you, I kept wondering? (Until my dad would tell me to go to sleep!!!!)

Now that we thought up the club, I feel better (only a little!!!!). We'll still be doing things together in a way.

I promise, promise that Stevie, Laura, and I will write to you every week. I'll make sure to tell you EVERYTHING, like if I get Mrs. Higgle or if I get a part in the third-and-fourth-grade play. And you can tell me the same things about Kansas. (I hope they don't have a Mrs. Higgle, though.)

That way we'll still be best friends no matter where we are.

Your Friend 4-Ever,

Meg

P.S. We'll miss you.

Stevie's letter was last. When Molly picked it up, her hands were shaking.

Dear Molly,

At least I spelled your name right. Meg says we have to write a letter today. Which is dumb 'cause we know you're gonna be here soon.

Anyway, I was thinking what to write, and all I could think about was my tooth. Remember when I lost it and I kept doing that funny noise with my tongue? Everybody kept saying I'd get used to having no tooth. But I never did (get used to it, I mean). Every time I ate something, I needed that tooth right up 'til the new one came in.

Same thing with my father moving away (even though I don't want a new one of those !!!). And now it's gonna be the same with you. I already decided not to walk by your house, or I'll close my eyes if I have to. A year is a long time not to look at your house.

Meg says you're gonna be here any second,
so I have to stop. But I want you to know
you are just like my tooth.

> *Your Friend 4-Ever,*
> *(and yours 'til the*
> *meatball bounces)*

STEVIE

P.S. We'll miss you.

Molly folded Stevie's letter and gently placed it in the box. A big tear plopped right down in the middle of it before she got the lid on. She swallowed hard and curled her toes for a very long time. Then she looked up at each of her friends. "I'm going to read these every single night before I go to bed," she whispered.

"While you're doing that out in Kansas, I'll write more letters here at home," Meg said, giving Molly a big teary hug.

"Me, too," Laura whispered, wiping her eyes with the hem of her T-shirt.

"Me, three," Stevie said, wrapping her arms

tight around Molly. "But not every single night, okay?"

The girls laughed and squeezed themselves into a small circle. Molly was going far away, but a little piece of her would always be there.

Without her best friend, Molly, what does Stevie do when she feels Meg and Laura are leaving her out of their fun? Read Friends 4-Ever #2, YOURS 'TIL THE MEATBALL BOUNCES.

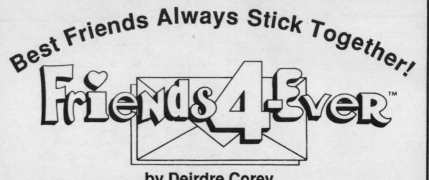